ZONDER**kidz**™

Freddie's Fast-Cash Getaway
Copyright © 2009 by Bill Myers
Illustrations © 2009 by Andy Smith

Requests for information should be addressed to:
Zonderkidz, Grand Rapids, Michigan 49530

Library of Congress Cataloging-in-Publication Data
Myers, Bill, 1953-
  Freddie's fast-cash getaway : the parable of the prodigal son / written by Bill Myers
; illustrated by Andy J. Smith.
      p. cm. -- (Bug parables)
  Summary: In this retelling of the parable of the prodigal son, Freddie the ant leaves
his family's worm farm for the city only to find that life there is not as he imagined, so
he humbles himself and returns home.
  ISBN 978-0-310-71218-3 (hardcover : alk. paper) [1. Stories in rhyme. 2. Ants--Fiction.
3. Insects--Fiction. 4. Prodigal son (Parable)--Fiction. 5. Parables--Fiction. 6. Christian
life--Fiction.] I. Smith, Andy J., 1975- II. Title.
  PZ8.3.M99534Fr 2009
  [E]--dc22
                                                    2008009445

Editor: Betsy Flikkema
Art direction & design: Sarah Molegraaf

Printed in China

09 10 11 12 • 5 4 3 2 1

FREDDIE'S FAST-CASH GETAWAY

The Parable of the Prodigal Son

THE BUG PARABLES

written by
BILL MYERS

illustrated by
ANDY J. SMITH

ZONDERkidz

ZONDERVAN.com/
AUTHORTRACKER
follow your favorite authors

The family worm farm
just isn't for Fred.
Life's glitz and its glamour
are what fill his head.

Next come the sideshows: bearded ladybugs and more.

FREAK SHOW

BEARDED LADY BUG

FANTASTIC 9 LEGGED SPIDER!

It's gonna cost cash if you want through this door.

Next come the wild rides.
He pays for that too.

By the time the sun rises his money's all gone...

and so are his friends.

That's it??

Well, so long!

And now all alone without even a dime,

McMaggot

maggot's

for Fred it's a drag when it comes to meal time.

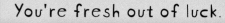

What was I thinking? I'm completely to blame.
So he hops a ride home on the very next train.
Quakey oatmeal
Nutrition Facts
ANTERCONTINENTAL RAIL

But Dad, he's been waiting
every day for his son,

checking the mailbox
since Fred's journey's begun.

They fire up the barbie
and throw more steaks down.

Let's throw a big party!
Let's invite the whole town!

They sing and rejoice
at young Freddie's return.

There's so much love here,
and none that I've earned.